Young Cam Jansen
and the
New Girl Mystery

BY **D**AVID **A.** **A**DLER

ILLUSTRATED BY **S**USANNA **N**ATTI

PUFFIN BOOKS

For Ethan, Juliet, and Fiona,
the newest generation in a reading, writing family
—D. A.

To my faraway cousins John, Tom, and Betty
—S. N.

PUFFIN BOOKS
Published by the Penguin Group
Penguin Young Readers Group, 345 Hudson Street, New York, New York 10014, U.S.A.
Penguin Group (Canada), 10 Alcorn Avenue, Toronto, Ontario, Canada M4V 3B2
(a division of Pearson Penguin Canada Inc.)
Penguin Books Ltd, 80 Strand, London WC2R 0RL, England
Penguin Ireland, 25 St Stephen's Green, Dublin 2, Ireland (a division of Penguin Books Ltd)
Penguin Group (Australia), 250 Camberwell Road, Camberwell, Victoria 3124, Australia
(a division of Pearson Australia Group Pty Ltd)
Penguin Books India Pvt Ltd, 11 Community Centre, Panchsheel Park, New Delhi - 110 017, India
Penguin Group (NZ), Cnr Airborne and Rosedale Roads, Albany, Auckland,
New Zealand (a division of Pearson New Zealand Ltd)
Penguin Books (South Africa) (Pty) Ltd, 24 Sturdee Avenue, Rosebank, Johannesburg 2196, South Africa

Registered Offices: Penguin Books Ltd, 80 Strand, London WC2R 0RL, England

First published in the United States of America by Viking,
a division of Penguin Young Readers Group, 2004

Published by Puffin Books, a division of Penguin Young Readers Group, 2005

9 10 8

THE LIBRARY OF CONGRESS HAS CATALOGED THE VIKING EDITION AS FOLLOWS:
Adler, David A.
Young Cam Jansen and the new girl mystery / by David A. Adler; illustrated by Susanna Natti.
p. cm.
Summary: This time Cam Jansen relies on her hearing rather than
her photographic memory to find a missing classmate.
ISBN: 0-670-05915-3 (hardcover)
[1. Schools—Fiction. 2. Mystery and detective stories.]
I. Natti, Susanna, ill. II. Title. PZ7.A2615Ys 2004 [Fic]—dc22 2003019768

Puffin Easy-to-Read ISBN 978-0-14-240353-2

Puffin® and Easy-to-Read® are registered trademarks of Penguin Group (USA) Inc.

Manufactured in China
Set in Bookman

Reading Level 2.0

CONTENTS

Cam Jansen has an amazing memory. Do you?

Look at this picture. Blink your eyes and say, "Click!" Then turn to the last page of this book.

1. "I'M WEARING DAD'S SOCKS"

"I can't find any of my things,"

Jenny said.

"Sh," Eric told her.

"My books and games

are all in boxes."

"Sh," Eric said again.

"I found the shirt I'm wearing

in a soup pot."

Eric turned.

He told Jenny,

"Ms. Dee doesn't want us

to talk in class."

Jenny was new in school.

She had just moved with her family

to a house on Eric's block.

Now she sat behind him in class.

"Where is it?" Ms. Dee asked.

She held a large book.

She turned a few pages.

"Where is it?" she asked again.

Ms. Dee turned a few more pages.

"Cam," she said,

"on what page is that picture

of Abraham Lincoln?"

"Do we have to know pages?" Jenny asked.

"I can't remember pages! I need to go back
to my old school."

Cam Jansen closed her eyes.

She said, "Click!"

"It's on page 29," Cam said.

Ms. Dee turned to page 29.

"Yes, here it is."

Ms. Dee showed the picture
to the class.

She told the class

about President Abraham Lincoln.

"I can't remember pages," Jenny said.

"I can't even remember

where I packed my socks."

Jenny stuck her feet out.

"Look," she told Eric.

"I'm wearing Dad's socks."

The socks hung over her sneakers.

"You don't have to remember pages,"

Eric told her.

"But you do have to be quiet."

Ms. Dee talked about President Lincoln,

and Eric listened.

"Eric," Jenny whispered.

"I have a question."

Eric looked straight ahead.

"I have a question," Jenny said again.

"How did that Cam girl

remember the page?"

Eric didn't answer.

He looked straight ahead

until it was time for lunch.

2. CLICK! CLICK! CLICK!

Eric told Jenny, "Now we can talk.

Now you can meet my friend Cam.

I'll tell you

how she remembered the page.

We can all eat lunch together,

and we can talk."

Cam, Eric, and Jenny

took their lunch bags from the closet.

Before they left the room,

Ms. Dee stopped them.

"Jenny," Ms. Dee said.

"After lunch, please go to gym."

"Okay."

"And please, don't talk in class."

Cam, Eric, and Jenny walked together
to the lunchroom.

"What about Cam's memory?"

Jenny asked.

Cam stopped.

She looked at Jenny and said, "Click!"

Then Cam closed her eyes.

Eric told Jenny,

"Cam's memory is like a camera.

She has pictures in her head

of everything she's seen.

Click! is the sound

the camera in her head makes

when it takes a picture."

"You have wavy brown hair,"

Cam said with her eyes still closed.

"You're wearing blue pants,

a red shirt, and floppy socks."

"These are my dad's socks," Jenny said.

"And you ate eggs this morning."

"Hey," Jenny said.

"How did you know about the eggs?"

"There's some on your shirt."

Eric said, "Cam's real name is Jennifer.

But because of her great memory

people called her 'The Camera.'

Then 'The Camera' became just Cam."

Jenny wiped the egg off her shirt.

Cam opened her eyes.

"Click! Click! Click!" Jenny said

as they walked to the lunchroom.

"My head is like a camera, too,"

Jenny said. "It's like a camera

without any film."

Jenny said, "Hey!"

to the two men

who stood by the lunchroom door.

"I'm new here. I'm Jenny."

One of the men said, "I'm Bill.

Please use trays

and clean your table

when you're done eating."

"I'm Jim," the other man said.

Cam, Eric, and Jenny

sat at a table by the window.

Danny sat at the table, too.

He stood, held an open book,

and turned pages.

Then he asked in a squeaky voice,

"Where are you President Lincoln?

Where are you President Lincoln?

You know it's not nice

to hide from the teacher."

Danny closed the book.

He laughed.

Jenny laughed, too.

"You sounded just like

Ms. Dee," she said.

Cam, Eric, and Danny ate.

Jenny talked and ate.

She talked and talked.

Cam finished eating.

She looked around the lunchroom.

"Oh, my!" she said. "I didn't hear the bell.

We have to hurry."

They cleaned their table

and went to gym.

"On your marks!" Mr. Day said.

"Let's stretch."

"Wait!" Eric said.

"Jenny is new here.

She doesn't have a mark."

Mr. Day looked at the children

standing on their marks.

"There's no one new here," he said.

"I know I'm not new," Danny said.

"I'm old, seven years old."

"Well, Jenny *is* new," Cam said.

"But where is she?

Where's Jenny?"

3. "THE BACK DOOR IS OPEN!"

Cam said,

"Maybe Jenny went back to class."

Eric said,

"Maybe she's lost."

Mr. Day told Cam and Eric

to look for Jenny.

Cam and Eric went into the hall.

"Maybe she went back to class,"

Eric said.

"Maybe she's talking to Ms. Dee."

"No," Cam said.

"If Jenny went to class,

Ms. Dee would tell her to go to gym."

"Let's look there anyway," Eric said.

Cam and Eric went to class.

The door was closed.

The lights were off.

"I think she's lost," Eric said.

Cam and Eric

walked through the school.

They searched the halls.

They looked in the lunchroom.

They didn't find Jenny.

"Look," Eric said, and pointed.

"The back door is open!

Maybe Jenny went outside."

Cam and Eric looked outside.

Lots of children

were in the playground.

Eric said, "Maybe Jenny

went to the wrong gym.

Maybe instead of Mr. Day's gym

she went to the jungle gym."

4. "JUST LET ME THINK"

Cam and Eric went outside.

It was a large playground.

Children were running

from one side of it to the other.

Children were on swings.

Some were on the jungle gym.

Three teachers were sitting on chairs.

They were watching the children.

Two children ran past Cam and Eric.

Two other children ran behind a tree.

"I can't see everyone," Eric said.

"And they don't keep still.

It would help if I remembered

what Jenny was wearing."

Cam closed her eyes.

She said, "Click!

She's wearing a red shirt,

blue pants, and floppy socks,"

Cam said with her eyes closed.

"Good," Eric said.

"I'll just look for someone

in a red shirt."

Cam opened her eyes.

Two girls ran past.

"They went by so fast," Eric said.

"I didn't see their faces.

But I did see their shirts.

And they are *not* wearing

red shirts."

Cam and Eric did find

a few children wearing red shirts.

But they didn't find Jenny.

Eric told Cam,

"In class Jenny said,

'I need to go back to my old school.'

Maybe that's what she did."

"No," Cam said.

"I'm sure her old school

is a long way from here."

Cam and Eric went inside.

"Let's look

in all the classes," Eric said.

"Let's look in the halls and bathrooms."

"No," Cam said. "Just let me think.

I need to remember something."

Eric said, "Just close your eyes

and say 'Click!'"

"No. Not this time," Cam told him.

"I don't need to remember

what I've seen.

I need to remember what I've heard."

She stood there and thought.

Then she said, "That's it!

You did it," she told Eric.

"You solved the mystery."

"I did?" Eric asked.

"Yes, you did," Cam said.

"Now let's get Jenny."

5. "HOW DID *I* SOLVE THE MYSTERY?"

Eric had to run

to keep up with Cam.

"How did *I* solve the mystery?"

Eric asked.

"And where are we going?"

"We're going right here,"

Cam said.

They were by the door

to the kitchen.

It was closed.

Cam knocked on the door.

"Ms. Dee told Jenny to go to gym.

You said there is more

than one gym in the school.

Well there is.

Jenny just went

to the wrong gym."

"But she didn't go

to the jungle gym,"

Eric said.

"I'm glad you think

I solved the mystery,

but it's still a mystery to me."

Bill opened the kitchen door.

Cam said, "We're looking for Jenny."

Bill said, "She's in the kitchen."

Jenny was helping Bill and Jim

wash the lunch trays.

"Why are you here?" Eric asked.

"Ms. Dee told her

to help me," Jim said.

"Last week I told Ms. Dee

I was working too hard.

And today she asked

Jenny to help me."

"Yes," Jenny said.

"She told me to go to Jim."

"She told you to go to gym," Cam said.

"G–Y–M *not* J–I–M!"

"Oh," Jenny said.

"You're a good helper," Bill said.

"And a good talker," Jim said.

Cam and Eric said,

"Now she has to go to gym."

"G–Y–M?" Jenny asked.

"Yes," Cam and Eric told her.

"G–Y–M!"

A Cam Jansen
Memory Game

Take another look at the picture on page 4.

Study it.

Blink your eyes and say, "Click!"

Then turn back to this page

and answer these questions:

1. What color is Cam's T-shirt?

2. How many children are in the picture?

3. Is Cam's book open or closed?

4. What is the animal of the week?

5. Eric's book is open. Is he reading it?